D0468316

# The Magic School Bus

## IN THE ARCTIC

### A BOOK ABOUT HEAT

SCHOLASTIC INC.

New York   Toronto   London   Auckland   Sydney
Mexico City   New Delhi   Hong Kong   Buenos Aires

From an episode of the animated TV series
produced by Scholastic Entertainment Inc.
Based on *The Magic School Bus* books
written by Joanna Cole and illustrated by Bruce Degen.

*TV tie-in adaptation by Anne Schreiber and illustrated by Art Ruiz.*
*TV script written by Brian Meehl, George Bloom, and Jocelyn Stevenson.*

ISBN 0-590-18724-4

24 23 22 21 20 19 18 17 16 15                                          4 5 6 7 8 9/0

Printed in the U.S.A.

Ms. Frizzle is the weirdest teacher in the school. Strange things always seem to happen in her class. But it had gotten to be so cold outside, not even Ms. Frizzle could do anything too unusual.

Or so we thought.

It all started in the cafeteria when Arnold ordered a steaming cup of hot cocoa with marshmallows. By the time he took his first sip, the heat had escaped out an open window. Arnold was left with yucky cold cocoa!

"Where did all the hot go?" he asked. That's when Ms. Frizzle got that snowy sparkle in her eyes.

The next thing we knew, we were on the Magic School Bus, but now it had skis and tractor treads instead of tires. We were traveling through one of the coldest places on Earth — the Arctic — and we didn't even have our coats on!

Ms. Frizzle pressed a button and jackets dropped from the top of the bus, but they were too thin to keep us warm. And while the Friz was searching for the warm jacket button, she drove the bus into deep, ice-cold water!

When we got to the other side, the bus was dripping with ice and the engine was frozen.

Then the bus just stopped, and we were STUCK IN THE ARCTIC!

We had to figure out a way to warm up the bus and get back home. We were cold, but poor Liz was freezing.

"Liz is cold-blooded. She gets most of her heat from outside her body," explained Phoebe as she tucked Liz inside her jacket. "Don't worry, Liz," she said. "I'm warm-blooded. My heat is your heat."

Just then, Wanda pulled out an old wooden trunk from under a seat. Inside we found a bunch of goggles. Ms. Frizzle said they were "heat peepers."

It was amazing. When we put them on, we could actually see heat moving out of our bodies.

"Moving heat must mean losing heat," said Phoebe. We could see the heat escaping right out of the top of the bus.

The heat was escaping fast. We needed a heat source. Luckily, Arnold found some wood inside the old trunk. In no time, a fire was burning, and Ms. Frizzle was cheerfully brewing hot lemon-water tea.

This fire is a very good source of heat.

This trip is really *heating* up!

The wood didn't last long, so we broke another wooden trunk into pieces. Out fell some hot-water bottles.

Ms. Frizzle poured tea into a hot-water bottle. With our heat peepers, we could see the heat going into it.

Carlos tucked the bottle inside his jacket. He felt warmer right away.

Arnold looked at the other hot-water bottles on the ground. "What if we cover the engine of the bus with hot-water bottles?" he suggested. "The heat from the bottles will move into the engine, the engine will warm up, the bus will start, and we can go home."

It was a good idea, but it was too late.

We had to save Ralphie and Phoebe, but we were freezing. "Look," said Carlos, "the heat from my hot-water bottle is almost gone."

"We have to find something else to keep ourselves warm," Arnold said. He looked at Dorothy Ann's book. "We could use that!"

Arnold started to rip out pages from the book and stuff them inside his jacket. "I hate to hurt a book, but this is an emergency."

"Putting this paper between us and the cold air might keep the heat from escaping," Arnold explained.

The paper did slow down the loss of heat a little bit. Ms. Frizzle said the paper was acting like insulation — it was holding in heat. But we still needed a better heat source if we were going to save the bus and get home.

"There's a fur coat and a heat source due north of here," said the Friz. "Follow me."

Ms. Frizzle was right. This heat source was warm, furry, and smelled like . . . fish. Suddenly, we got it. This was no ordinary heat source. This was a POLAR BEAR!

"Run!" said Carlos.

"Hide!" said Tim.

"Oh bad, oh bad, oh bad," said Keesha.

Ms. Frizzle came to the rescue. She whipped out the porta-shrinker and *zap* — we were as small as a bee's knees.

We whirled into the bear's fur.

We were tiny but warm. We could see the heat coming out of the polar bear's body and getting trapped by its thick, tangled fur. The fur kept in the heat, just like the paper under our jackets kept in our body heat.

Suddenly, our polar bear got itchy. We tried to hang on, but we couldn't. It was time to make tracks.

Back on the bus, Phoebe and Ralphie were pretty cold. Phoebe searched the bus for blankets. But when she reached inside the blanket compartment, she came out with a handful of gloopy blubber.

"What kind of blanket is this?" asked Phoebe.

"It's a fat blanket," said Ralphie, looking through his heat peepers. "And it sure can keep in the heat."

This blanket is as soft as butter.

It's one hundred percent fat.

Suddenly, the bus tipped dangerously. Ralphie and Phoebe looked out and saw walruses trying to climb onto the ice floe!

"Is it just me, or are those walruses floating in freezing cold water without losing much body heat?" Phoebe asked. "And they don't have thick fur like polar bears."

"I'll bet all that blubber in their bodies traps their heat — just like the fat on your hand," Ralphie said.

"If it's good enough for a walrus, it's good enough for us," said Phoebe. Then she and Ralphie covered themselves from head to toe in gloopy fat.

But Phoebe and Ralphie weren't out of cold water yet. Their ice floe was breaking apart — and we couldn't reach them!

"We have to save them," said Keesha.

"But we won't last in that icy water," said Dorothy Ann.

"Never fear," said the Friz. "Where there's a Liz, there's a way." She gave a whistle, then called out, "Hit it, Liz!"

Uh-oh. I think the Friz has an idea.

Liz ran into the bus and pulled a lever on the dashboard. Suddenly, the roof of the bus opened and something came flying across the water right at us.

We swam for the bus. We felt warm in our blubber suits.

We were glad to be back together. But we still had to find a way to warm up the bus so we could get back home.

We tried exercising. The heat escaping from our bodies melted the fat and warmed up the bus — for a while. Then the heat escaped out the top of the bus.

"We need something to trap the heat and keep it inside," Arnold said.

Luckily, the bus had special igloo-building equipment. So we built an igloo around the bus to trap escaping heat. Ms. Frizzle explained that the snow on the igloo can trap heat because snow is filled with tiny air pockets. The heat moves into these air pockets and gets blocked.

As soon as our igloo was built, we went back to exercising. It was a big workout. The heat from our bodies was kept inside the igloo, so the bus started to warm up. Before you could say, "jumping jack," the engine was ready to go, and we put the blubber to the road.

We were just in time. Ms. Frizzle turned the bus into a helicopter and got us out of there just before the ice floe broke into tiny pieces.

Back at home, Arnold ordered another nice mug of hot cocoa. But this time, he wasn't going to let the heat escape. He wrapped up his drink in a home-made, double-layered, zipper-lidded, quilted cocoa-cozy.

Well, as Ms. Frizzle always says, "Ah, the inspiration of insulation!"

I see Arnold's got another hot drink.

And this time, it's going to stay hot.

# Letters to the Friz

Dear Ms. Frizzle,
I don't get why the kids had to be blubberized when all they had to do was wear wet suits.
From,
I.M. Freezing

Dear I.M.,
Wet suits contain millions of tiny air pockets that trap the heat and keep people warm in cold water. But we think blubber is better. Stay warm.
Love,
Ms. Frizzle

Dear Ms. Frizzle,
Those heat peepers were cool. Where can I get a pair?
Your friend,
Seymour Heat

Dear Seymour,
Sorry. Heat peepers are magic. You can't usually see heat move from place to place, but you can feel it.
Get messy,
The Friz

Dear Kids,
How could you let Ms. Frizzle take Liz to the Arctic? Everyone knows that cold-blooded animals can't survive in such cold climates.
Speaking for the lizards,
Rhett Tile

Dear Rhett,
Thanks for your concern. While it's usually true that you shouldn't take lizards to the Arctic, Liz is MAGIC!
Later,
The Kids

To Carlos,
When does snow hold things together?
When it's an i-glue.
Get it?
Joe King

Dear Kids,
I hope you come to visit us again soon. Next time, wear your jackets.
Sincerely,
Art Tic

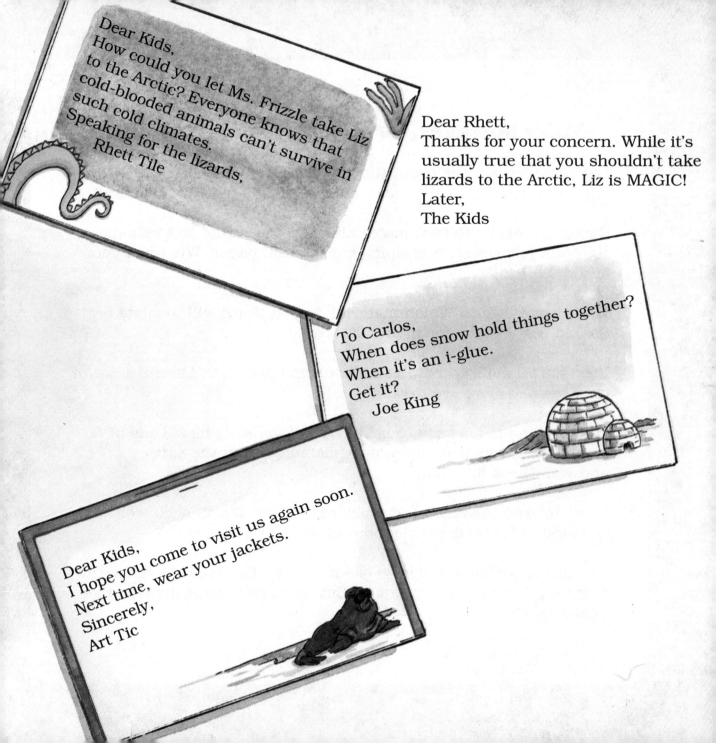

# Make Mistakes, Get Messy, Try This at Home

Did you ever wonder about the inspiration for insulation? Try this experiment to find out which material makes the best heat trap.

Choose several different materials. Here are some suggestions: cotton, a pillowcase, a sleeping bag, tinfoil, paper. What are your ideas?

Make a prediction. Which material do you think will insulate best? Second best? Write down your guesses.

Now ask an adult to help you toast some bread. Toast one slice for each material you are testing.

When the toast is ready, quickly wrap each slice inside one of the insulators. Keep each piece of insulated toast in the same place and wait three minutes.

Now, unwrap the toast and touch each slice. Which slice feels the warmest? Was your prediction correct?

Try this experiment again to see if you get the same result. Write down what happens each time. (But don't go outside dressed in a pillowcase!)